Neil Gaiman
Chu's Day
at the Beach

Illustrated By Adam Rex

HARPER
An Imprint of HarperCollinsPublishers

For Eve Gonson, a perfect audience.
—N.G.

For Henry.
—A.R.

Chu's Day at the Beach
Text copyright © 2015 by Neil Gaiman
Illustrations copyright © 2015 by Adam Rex
All rights reserved. Manufactured in China.
No part of this book may be used or reproduced in any manner whatsoever without written
permission except in the case of brief quotations embodied in critical articles and reviews. For information address
HarperCollins Children's Books, a division of HarperCollins Publishers, 195 Broadway, New York, NY 10007.
www.harpercollinschildrens.com

ISBN 978-0-06-222399-9

The artist used oil and mixed media on board to create the illustrations for this book.
Typography by Alison Carmichael
15 16 17 18 19 SCP 10 9 8 7 6 5 4 3 2 1
❖
First Edition

When Chu sneezed,

big things happened.

It was a hot day, and Chu and his family went to the beach.

Chu had an ice cream. The ice-cream
seller was very nice. She gave Chu an
extra scoop of vanilla.

Chu said hello
to a crab in a rock pool.
Chu's mother sat on the sand
and read her book. Chu's father
went into the water up to
his tummy.

Chu took off his sunglasses. He looked at
the sea. The day was so sunny and bright.

Chu's nose tickled.

It was a tickling that got bigger and
bigger and bigger.

It was a tickling that filled his whole head. . . .

AAH-

AAAAH-

AAAAAH-

"Uh-oh,"
said Chu.

"Chu," said Chu's mother.

"Chu!" said Chu's father. "What did you DO?"

All the people on the beach went down to look.

Chu said hello to some fish. The fish looked at him. They looked sad.

He waved at a family
of merpandas. The
littlest merpanda
waved back at him.

Chu saw a whale.

The whale was very big.
"With the sea broken, I
cannot go home," said
the whale.

"You must put this back the way
it was," said the ice-cream seller.
"Or nobody will come
to the beach
anymore, and
they will not
eat my
ice cream."

Please sneeze again, Chu.
But Chu could not sneeze.

A seagull tickled Chu's
nose with a feather.
"Will you sneeze?"
said the seagull.

AAH.

AAAAH.

AAAAAH.

"No," said Chu.

"Perhaps a bubbly drink will make you sneeze," said the ice-cream seller. She gave Chu a fizzy drink, with bubbles that went up Chu's nose.

Please sneeze again, Chu. Will you sneeze now?

AAH.

AAAAH.

AAAAAH.

"No," said Chu.

All of the grown-ups were very sad.
"Chu will not sneeze," they said.
"Now the sea is broken and
we cannot fix it."

Then Tiny the snail climbed up to Chu's ear and whispered, "Sometimes I sneeze when I see the sun."

Chu took off his sunglasses.

AAAA

"There," said Chu. "Everything is back just as it was before."

The ice-cream seller was so pleased,
she gave Chu another ice cream.

In the sea, Chu saw a merpanda
just his size. She swam over to him.

"Sometimes I sneeze too," she said.
And then she swam away.

"There," said Chu. "Everything is back just as it was before."

The ice-cream seller was so pleased,
she gave Chu another ice cream.

In the sea, Chu saw a merpanda
just his size. She swam over to him.

"Sometimes I sneeze too," she said.
And then she swam away.

"Did you have a nice day at the beach?" asked Chu's mother and father.

"I had the best day at the beach," said Chu, holding his seagull feather.

Goodnight.